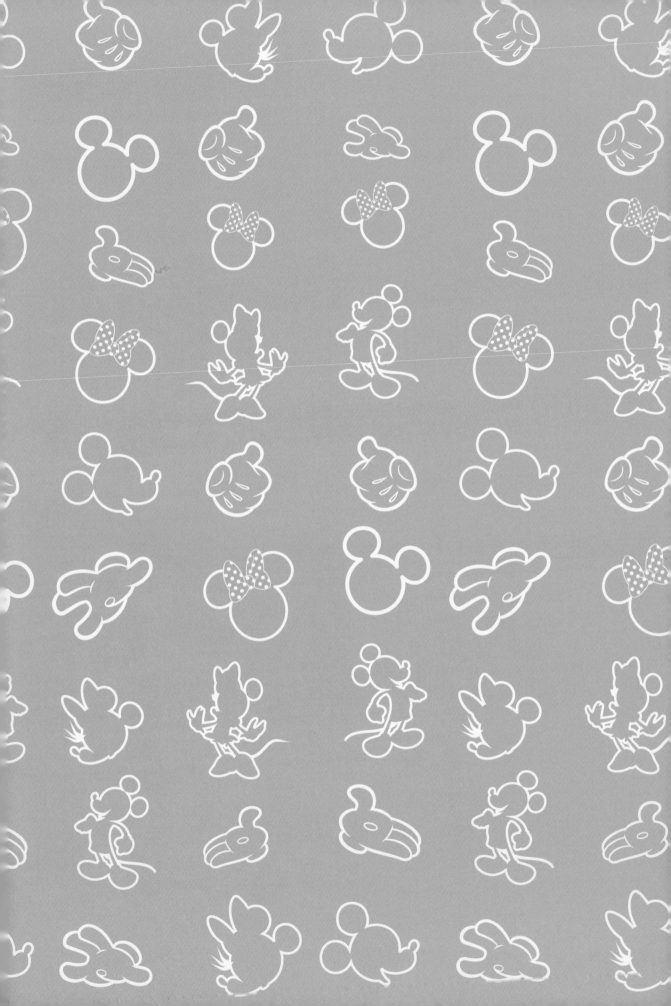

Disney

To:
_____

From:
_____

Studio Fun International
An imprint of Printers Row Publishing Group
A division of Readerlink Distribution Services, LLC
10350 Barnes Canyon Road, Suite 100, San Diego, CA 92121
www.studiofun.com

Printers Row Publishing Group is a division of Readerlink Distribution Services, LLC.
Studio Fun International is a registered trademark of Readerlink Distribution Services, LLC.

Let's Go to the Fire House based on the story by Lucy Geist. Illustrated by DiCicco Digital Arts.
Minnie's Scavenger Hunt based on the story by Kate Ritchey. Illustrated by the Disney Storybook Art Team.
Dairy Farm Doozie based on the story by Barbara Buzaldua. Illustrated by Sue DiCicco.
Where's Fifi? based on the story by Lyn Calder. Illustrated by Adam DeVaney.
The Flower Prowler based on the story by Catherine Hapka. Illustrated by Sue DiCicco.
The Butterscotch Bandit based on the story by Catherine Hapka. Illustrated by Sue DiCicco.
Ticket Trouble based by Catherine Hapka. Illustrated by Sue DiCicco.
A Perfect Picnic based on the story by Kate Ritchey. Illustrated by the Disney Storybook Art Team.
The Campout Washout based on the book by Megan Bryant. Illustrated by the Disney Storybook Art Team.
Mickey and the Pet Shop based on the book by Mary Packard.
The Kitten Sitters based on the book by Megan Bryant. Illustrated by the Disney Storybook Art Team.
A Surprise for Pluto based on the book by Ellie O'Ryan.
A Summer Day based on the story by Kate Ritchey. Illustrated by the Disney Storybook Art Team.
The Bravest Dog based on the story "The Bravest Dog."

Cover designed by Kara Kenna
Designed by Judy O Productions, Inc.

All notations of errors or omissions should be addressed to Studio Fun International, Editorial Department, at the above address.

ISBN: 978-0-7944-4434-1

Manufactured, printed, and assembled in Heshan, China.
Second printing, December 2019. LP/12/19
23 22 21 20 19   2 3 4 5 6

Disney

Stories

for

2-Year-Olds

studio fun
INTERNATIONAL

TABLE OF CONTENTS

LET'S GO TO THE FIREHOUSE

Donald's nephews and Mickey were on their way to the firehouse. They were going to decorate an old fire truck for a parade.

Donald was working on a top-secret float by himself.

Goofy and Mickey were junior volunteer firefighters. Mickey polished the truck as the boys decorated it.

Mickey explained that the old fire truck was perfect for parades, but wasn't as powerful as newer fire trucks.

Mickey showed the boys a new fire truck's powerful pump and hoses.

"It must be hard work being a firefighter," said Louie.

"It sure is," Goofy responded.

Goofy told a story about saving Mrs. Porter's bird from a burning building.

"I thought the firefighters rescued the bird and had you hold it," said Mickey.

"But I was a big help," Goofy said.
"I gave the bird back to Mrs. Porter!"

13

Goofy told another story about a campfire that roared out of control. But Mickey remembered that he and Goofy only passed out blankets while the firefighters put out the fire.

Goofy decided to stop telling
stories. He and the others finished
decorating and headed home together.

The next day, the gang rode in the fire truck in the parade.

"We're going to win the blue ribbon for best parade entry!" exclaimed Louie.

Uncle Donald's super-secret float rode along in the parade. His float had a rocket mounted on it. Suddenly, sparks from the rocket went flying and the rocket caught on fire!

"Help! Fire!" yelled Donald.

"I'll save you!" exclaimed Goofy.
Goofy used the fire truck's hose to
put out the fire.

Goofy was a hero at last! After the parade, the mayor gave Goofy a blue ribbon for saving the day!

THE CAMPOUT WASHOUT

M‌ickey and his friends were going on a camping trip.

They packed up their camping supplies in Mickey's little red car. The friends drove up a mountain to the woods.

Mickey parked next to a lake.

"What should we do first?"
asked Goofy.

"Let's set up the tents," said Mickey.

Daisy and Minnie began setting up the tents.

"Mickey, where are the tent poles?"
Minnie asked.

Oh no! Mickey had forgotten them.

It started getting dark so Mickey
wanted to build a campfire. They
could sleep next to it to keep warm.

Back at camp, Goofy made a
circle of rocks then piled up sticks.

"I'll light the fire," said Goofy, patting his pockets.

"Aw, shucks," he said "I forgot to bring matches!"

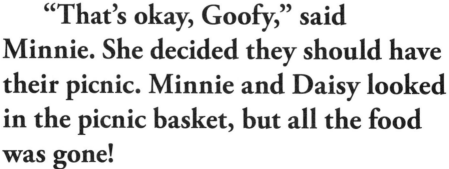

"That's okay, Goofy," said
Minnie. She decided they should have
their picnic. Minnie and Daisy looked
in the picnic basket, but all the food
was gone!

Everyone was hungry. The friends
didn't have tents, a fire, or food!

Suddenly, lightning flashed and it started to rain. "Maybe we should go home," Mickey said.

**Mickey felt he had let his friends
down. Then, Mickey had an idea!**

Back at Mickey's house,
he suggested they camp in his
living room.

"What a great idea!" said Minnie.

They made a fire in the fireplace, built tents, and ate a picnic in Mickey's cozy house. "This is the best camping trip ever!" they exclaimed.

MICKEY AND THE PET SHOP

Mr. Palmer was going on a trip, so Mickey was looking after Mr. Palmer's pet shop.

"Have a good time!" called Mickey.

All of the pets seemed happy except for one puppy. Mickey decided the puppy needed some attention.

Mickey lifted the puppy from the kennel. The puppy wriggled free and raced over to the fishbowl.

The puppy knocked the fishbowl over. The fish flopped through the air. Mickey caught the fish and put it back in its bowl.

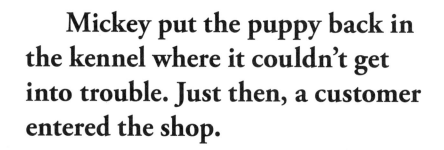

Mickey put the puppy back in
the kennel where it couldn't get
into trouble. Just then, a customer
entered the shop.

Suddenly, the puppy got out and opened the door to a cage of mice.

"Eek! I'll come back later," the customer said, running out the door.

That night, the puppy howled.
Mickey covered his ears with a
pillow, but it didn't help.

Soon, the puppy got what he wanted—a cozy spot in the bed next to Mickey.

The next day, the puppy was making even more messes in the pet shop.

As Mickey worked, the puppy followed him.

"You may be a rascal, but I am getting used to having you around," said Mickey.

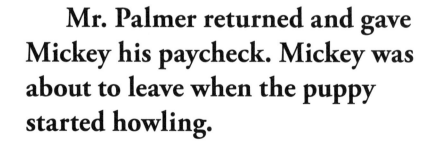

Mr. Palmer returned and gave
Mickey his paycheck. Mickey was
about to leave when the puppy
started howling.

Mickey went over to the puppy's kennel and said, "I'm going to miss you too, little fella."

Mickey had an idea! He used his paycheck to buy the puppy.

Mickey decided to name the
puppy Pluto. From then on, Mickey
and Pluto were best friends.

A PERFECT PICNIC

One day, Mickey called his friends and invited them to a picnic in the park.

Everyone would bring lunch to share. Mickey packed a yummy picnic lunch. He packed Pluto's favorite bones, too!

**Minnie filled her picnic basket
with all of her favorite foods. As she
got ready to leave, she wondered what
foods her friends had packed.**

She liked her food so much, she
didn't want to have to share.

Donald, Daisy, and Goofy felt the same way. They all loved their food. Maybe it was better to not share after all.

Mickey didn't know that his friends weren't planning on sharing. He filled his wagon and walked to the park with Pluto.

When he got to the park, he found his friends waiting for him. They all had picnic baskets, but they didn't look happy.

"What's wrong?" asked Mickey.

"I don't want to share my lunch," said Donald.

The other friends agreed.

Mickey was disappointed. Minnie saw how sad Mickey was, so she decided to trade lunches with him. Mickey's friends saw how happy Minnie had made Mickey.

They all decided to trade lunches,
too! The friends set out a picnic
blanket and passed out plates.

Mickey laughed when he saw what was inside Minnie's basket. Minnie looked in Mickey's basket and laughed, too. Everyone had packed peanut butter sandwiches with lemonade!

Everyone had brought different fruit.
Mickey made a fruit salad to share.
The friends realized that sharing was
fun after all!

THE FLOWER PROWLER

One spring day, Daisy brought Minnie flowers to plant in her garden. Minnie thought they'd look great with her daffodils.

The friends went in the backyard and found a big surprise. All of Minnie's daffodils were gone.

"It must be a flower prowler," said Daisy.

Daisy picked up a few strands of fuzzy, white hair. "Look! This could be a clue," said Daisy.

Ding, dong! Minnie answered
the door. Mickey was standing on the
front porch holding a bouquet
of daffodils.

"Hi Minnie," he said shyly.
"I brought you a present," he said.

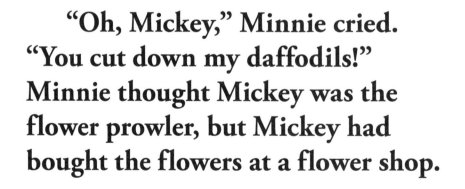

"Oh, Mickey," Minnie cried.
"You cut down my daffodils!"
Minnie thought Mickey was the
flower prowler, but Mickey had
bought the flowers at a flower shop.

Minnie, Mickey, and Daisy
decided to look for the flower prowler.
They found Goofy at the park with a
daffodil pinned to his shirt.

Was Goofy the flower prowler? Goofy told Minnie that he bought the daffodil from Mr. Power's flower shop.

They went to the flower shop
and found Mr. Power surrounded
by daffodils. Mr. Power said his
daffodils came from a farmer
named Mrs. Pote.

Minnie and her friends went
to Mrs. Pote's farm. Mrs. Pote said
that her goat, Flower, sometimes ate
her daffodils.

That gave Minnie an idea. Minnie asked Mrs. Pote if she could see Flower.

Mrs. Pote led Minnie and her
friends to Flower's pen, but Flower
was gone! Minnie spotted footprints
leading out through the broken fence.

The friends followed the footprints until they got to Minnie's yard. Flower was happily eating the daffodils.

"There's our flower prowler," Minnie laughed.

THE KITTEN SITTERS

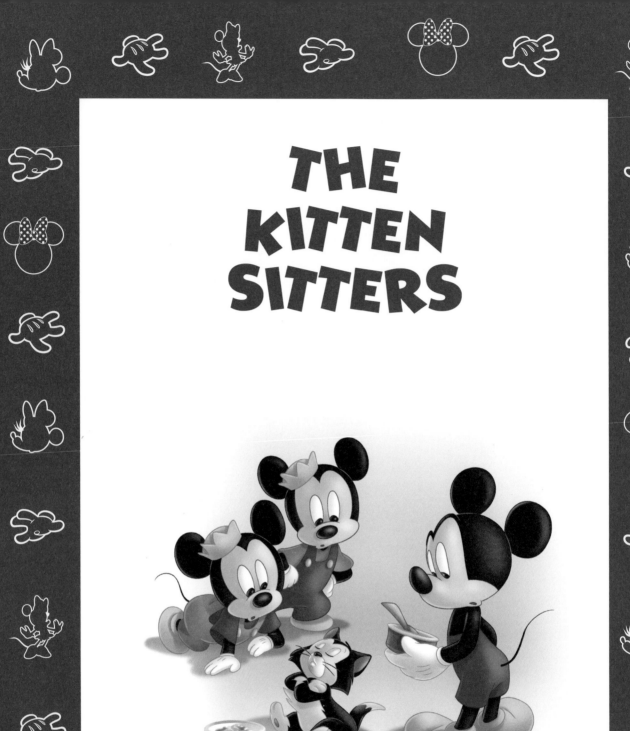

One day, Mickey told his nephews, Morty and Ferdie, that Minnie was going on a trip.

"We're going to look after her kitten, Figaro," said Mickey. The boys were very excited!

Cluck, cluck! An angry rooster chased Pluto through the backyard. Minnie scolded Pluto because she thought Pluto had chased the rooster.

"It's a good thing Figaro is staying with you," Minnie said to Mickey. "Maybe he can teach Pluto how to behave."

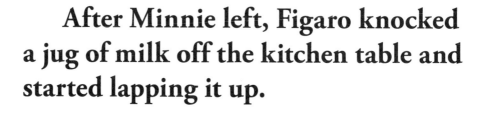

After Minnie left, Figaro knocked
a jug of milk off the kitchen table and
started lapping it up.

Later, Pluto ate all of his food like a good dog. Figaro wouldn't touch the special food that Minnie left for him.

When Mickey and his nephews went to bed, Mickey made a bed on the floor for Figaro. But he wanted Mickey's cozy bed instead.

Then, Figaro ran out of the
bedroom into the kitchen. Mickey
went after him and found the window
open. Figaro had run away!

Pluto and Mickey searched all over town for Figaro. A police officer said that he'd seen Figaro chasing ducks at the park.

Then a delivery man told Mickey that Figaro knocked over all of his eggs. Mickey and Pluto kept searching until sunrise.

Minnie arrived home, but Figaro was nowhere in sight.

Cluck, cluck! The chickens in the yard were being chased again— by Figaro!

"I'd hoped Figaro would teach Pluto some manners," Minnie said, marching away. Minnie thought Pluto taught Figaro to chase chickens!

Ferdie and Morty insisted that Figaro was naughty, not Pluto! Minnie and Figaro went home, giving Mickey, Pluto, and the boys some peace and quiet!

TICKET TROUBLE

M innie, Mickey, and Goofy were at the airport, ready to go on vacation.

"This is my very first time on an airplane!" exclaimed Goofy, "I even wore a pilot's hat for the trip!" he said.

Goofy decided to hide his ticket inside his pilot's hat.

A group of pilots walked down
the terminal and a breeze caused
Goofy's hat to fly off.

Goofy bumped into the pilots, knocking off their hats, too.

The pilots grabbed their hats off the ground.

When Goofy looked under his hat,
the ticket was gone! One of the pilots
had accidently taken Goofy's hat.

Mickey went to the air traffic control tower. "Can you please use your radios to ask the pilots if they have Goofy's hat and ticket?" Mickey asked.

Meanwhile, Goofy walked onto
the edge of the airfield. A plane slowly
drove by before taking off.

Goofy spotted a pilot driving a plane with his same hat. "Stop!" yelled Goofy.

The controller radioed the pilots about Goofy's missing hat. More and more airplanes surrounded Goofy. Soon the whole airport was at a standstill.

One of the pilots heard the
message. "I've got your hat! Come
and get it," said the pilot to Goofy.
Goofy looked inside the hat and
found his ticket.

The friends boarded the plane. Mickey gave Goofy his return ticket. "Don't worry," said Goofy. "This time I'm putting it in a safe place— my shoe!"

DAIRY FARM DOOZIE

Mickey, Donald, and Donald's nephews were at Grandma Duck's dairy farm. They were taking care of her cows while she was on vacation.

Mickey read Grandma's instructions for taking care of the cows.

"I know all of that," Donald said, walking toward the pasture.

The friends needed to lead the cows to the barn. One cow and calf didn't want to leave the pasture, so Donald tried to get their attention.

"This must be Rosie and her calf," said Mickey. "Grandma mentioned them in her instructions."

The instructions said to take
Rosie's calf to the barn and give it a
bottle. Donald tried to lead the calf,
but Rosie blocked the way.

Donald pushed and shoved Rosie, but she wouldn't budge. Soon, Rosie was so mad at Donald that she chased him while Mickey and the boys happily fed the calf.

After escaping Rosie, Donald joined Mickey and the boys as they gave the cows a bath.

"Who ever heard of washing a cow?" said Donald.

Donald tried milking Rosie,
but milk sprayed all over him.
Taking care of cows was harder
than Donald thought.

Later, Grandma Duck came home. She missed her cows too much to go on vacation.

"I hope I never have to see another cow again," grumbled Donald.

"That's too bad," said Grandma Duck.

Grandma Duck gave each of them a chocolate shaped like a cow!

WHERE'S FIFI?

One sunny day, Minnie was walking her dog Fifi when she saw a sign about a dog show.

"Oh look, Fifi," said Minnie. "A dog show with prizes—you should enter!"

Minnie and Fifi went home to
practice for the show. Minnie taught
Fifi how to sit and shake.

"Good dog, Fifi!" Minnie said proudly. When Minnie said roll over, Fifi barked. "No, you're supposed to bark when I say speak," said Minnie.

On the morning of the dog show, Minnie gave Fifi a bath and dressed her in a red polka dot bow.

"Now we match!" said Minnie.

As they walked down the street, Fifi saw a squirrel. Her leash slipped out of Minnie's hand and Fifi ran after the squirrel.

"Fifi! Come back!" yelled Minnie.
Minnie raced after Fifi, but she was
nowhere in sight.

Minnie called Daisy to tell her
Fifi was lost. Daisy said she'd call
Mickey to help find Fifi, too.

Daisy and Mickey found Minnie crying outside her house.

"Don't worry, Minnie. We'll find Fifi," promised Mickey.

Minnie and Mickey made missing signs for Fifi.

Suddenly, someone messaged
Daisy a picture of Fifi wearing a blue
ribbon. Fifi was at the dog show!

The dog show judge told Minnie
that Fifi was able to sit and shake
on command so she won the prize.
Minnie giggled and hugged Fifi.

A SURPRISE FOR PLUTO

One morning, Mickey looked out the window. "What a beautiful day to build something!" exclaimed Mickey.

Mickey told his nephews Morty and Ferdie that he was going to build a treehouse.

"A treehouse?" they exclaimed.

"Can we help?" Ferdie asked.

"Why don't you take Pluto to the park instead?" said Mickey.

"Sure, Uncle Mickey!"
they responded.

Mickey and his friends gathered in the backyard.

Goofy would cut boards while Donald and Mickey nailed them together.

Minnie showed Mickey a drawing of a plan she had for the treehouse.

"Good idea, Minnie!" said Mickey.

Minnie asked Goofy if he could
help cut some boards for her.

Goofy looked at Minnie's drawing and cut her some boards.

Mickey and Donald built
a sturdy rope ladder for the
tree. Goofy brought over a
stack of boards.

"Here you go!" said Goofy.

Everyone was busy painting, hammering, and sawing.

Later that day, Morty, Ferdie, and Pluto came back from the park.

"That's the best treehouse ever!" they exclaimed.

Pluto looked at the rope ladder; he was sad that he couldn't climb it.

"Come to the other side of the treehouse, Pluto," said Mickey.

Minnie had designed special stairs just for Pluto. Pluto ran up the stairs and joined his friends. It was the best treehouse ever!

129

THE BUTTERSCOTCH BANDIT

"Yummy!" Minnie said. She had baked a batch of butterscotch brownies for Daisy's party.

Minnie wrapped the brownies in foil and put them in a pretty pink shopping bag.

When Minnie got to Daisy's house, all of her friends were already there. Goofy was wearing bandages on both thumbs.

"I was trying to hang up some pictures," explained Goofy. "I sorta missed ... twice."

Minnie and Mickey started to dance.
After some time, Minnie remembered
her butterscotch brownies.

"I forgot to unpack my brownies," said Minnie.

"Yum! Let's eat them," said Goofy.

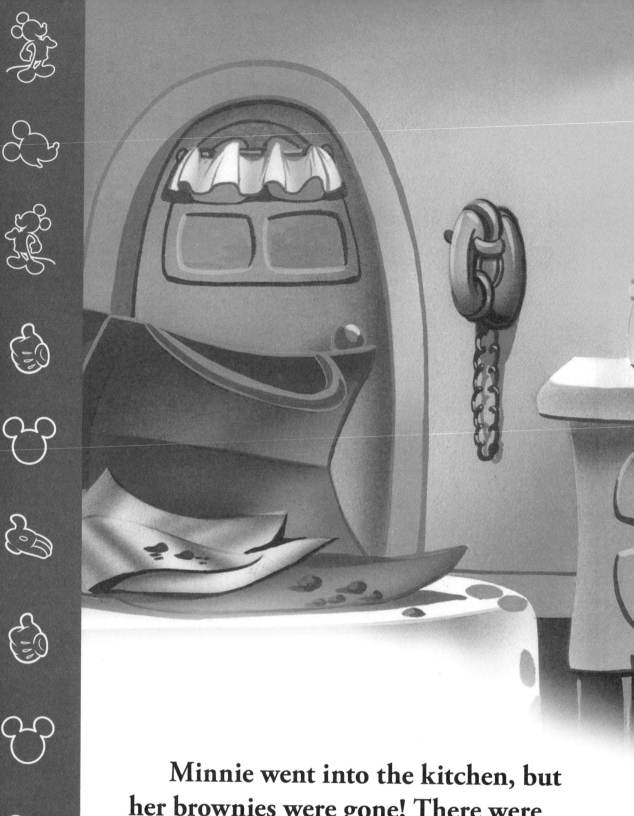

Minnie went into the kitchen, but her brownies were gone! There were only crumbs left.

"My brownies are missing!" cried Minnie.

"I haven't seen them," said Mickey, Daisy, and Donald.

"I wish I had," said Goofy. "But I haven't."

"Well, someone must have taken them," said Minnie. "One of you must have eaten them."

Daisy didn't like butterscotch, so it couldn't have been her. Mickey was dancing with Minnie so it couldn't have been him. Goofy had bandages on his thumbs so he couldn't have grabbed the brownies.

Donald looked more and more nervous. "It wasn't me!" he squawked.

The friends went to the kitchen and looked for clues. If they didn't eat the brownies, then who did?

They followed footprints into Daisy's bedroom. Pluto was sitting with butterscotch crumbs all around him.

"Don't be too hard on him, Mickey," said Minnie. "It looks like Pluto's already paying for his crime—with a tummy ache!"

A SUMMER DAY

It was a hot summer day. Mickey and his friends were relaxing inside his house when suddenly the air-conditioner broke!

The friends decided to go outside in hopes of a breeze. But there was no breeze—it was still too hot.

"Those sprinklers look nice and cool!" said Goofy.

"But there isn't enough water to keep us all cool," said Donald.

Suddenly, Minnie had an idea. "Let's go to the lake!"

The friends raced home to pack, and in no time, they were on their way to the lake.

Everyone had a different idea
of what activity to do first. Daisy
wanted to play basketball, Mickey
and Pluto wanted to play fetch, and
Donald wanted to go fishing.

Before anyone could stop him, Donald raced off toward a little boat docked beside the water.

"Donald, I don't think we can all fit in the boat," said Minnie. Minnie suggested they swim in the lake instead.

Everyone ran on the dock and
jumped into the lake for a swim.

Donald was the first to dive into the lake. It was so refreshing on a hot day!

"Ahh, you were right, Minnie. Swimming was a good idea," said Donald.

Minnie was happy she and her
friends had found a way to cool off.

Minnie and her friends got out of the water. Minnie had one last surprise for her friends . . . s'mores!

The friends gathered around a campfire and roasted marshmallows.

As the stars came out, the
gang put out their campfire
and decided it was time to leave.

Minnie and her friends packed their bags and got into the car.

"That was so much fun!"
said Donald. "Let's do it
again tomorrow!"

MINNIE'S SCAVENGER HUNT

One morning, Minnie found an envelope with a note. It was a secret scavenger hunt!

The first item on the list was a picnic basket. Minnie grabbed her basket and headed outside.

The next item on the list was
three cucumbers. She went into her
garden and picked the cucumbers.
The next item on the list was a stick.
Minnie headed for the woods.

She ran into Goofy in the woods. He was hiding blueberries behind his back. Minnie wondered if he was doing a secret scavenger hunt, too.

Minnie found a stick. Then she picked strawberries, the next item on the list.

Next, Minnie needed to find
five smooth stones. She waded in
the stream and picked up the stones.

165

The last thing Minnie needed was one yellow flower. Minnie started looking, but soon she was lost in the woods!

Minnie saw a trail of blueberries on the ground. She wondered if they were Goofy's. She followed the blueberries to a patch of yellow flowers.

Minnie picked a yellow flower, the last item on the list. She put it in her basket, then followed the path.

Minnie arrived at the park. Her friends were there carrying picnic baskets, too.

"Surprise!" exclaimed Mickey. Mickey had planned a scavenger hunt for his friends. They could use the items to throw a party in the park.

The friends had a picnic and played in the park all afternoon. It was a wonderful party and a perfect spring day!

THE BRAVEST DOG

I t was a beautiful, sunny day. Minnie was relaxing outside when Mickey ran out of his house.

He told Minnie that a circus train was going through town and one of the animals was missing. The sheriff needed Mickey's help finding it.

Pluto stayed with Minnie while Mickey searched for the circus animal.

After Mickey left, Pluto tugged on Minnie's skirt. Minnie decided it was a nice day to take Pluto for a walk by the river.

Pluto heard a hiss behind a log. Could it be a circus snake?

Pluto pounced behind the log, but it was just a cat and her kittens.

"It would be fun to find
a bear cub," said Minnie. "Or
a seal. I love seals! I wonder if
one could come this far."

Minnie and Pluto heard a splash in the river. Pluto raced down the hill and jumped in the water. "Be careful, Pluto!" exclaimed Minnie.

179

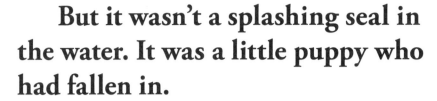

But it wasn't a splashing seal in the water. It was a little puppy who had fallen in.

Minnie laughed, the only
wild animals they found were
a puppy and kitten!

When Minnie and Pluto walked back into Mickey's kitchen, they found spilled milk and broken dishes.

Minnie wondered if a circus animal made the mess. Pluto sniffed around the kitchen, then leapt out of the window to the woodshed in the backyard.

"Be careful, Pluto!" cried Minnie.
"It could be dangerous!"

Just then, Mickey joined Minnie
in the backyard. Minnie told Mickey
about the mess in the kitchen.

After a few seconds, Pluto walked
out of the woodshed with a tiny
monkey on his back. The monkey
was wearing a little hat and vest.

"Pluto, you did it!" said Mickey.
"You found the missing circus animal!"

The playful monkey jumped into Mickey's arms.

Mickey laughed, "Maybe this little guy isn't so wild after all."

Pluto, Minnie, and Mickey returned the monkey to the circus ringmaster. "Thanks, Pluto," said the ringmaster. "The show couldn't have gone on without you!"

THE END